The Giant Jumperee

For Josephine Julia – J. D.

For Lily – H. O.

Dial Books for Young Readers
Penguin Young Readers Group
An imprint of Penguin Random House LLC
375 Hudson Street
New York, NY 10014

Text copyright © 2017 by Julia Donaldson
Illustrations copyright © 2017 by Helen Oxenbury
Originally published in the United Kingdom by Penguin Random House, 2017
First published in the United States 2017 by Dial Books for Young Readers

Library of Congress Cataloging-in-Publication Data

Names: Donaldson, Julia, author. | Oxenbury, Helen, illustrator.
Title: The Giant Jumperee / Julia Donaldson ; illustrated by Helen Oxenbury.
Description: New York, NY : Dial Books for Young Readers, [2017] | Summary: A baby
frog scares the other animals.
Identifiers: LCCN 2016016406 | ISBN 9780735227972 (hardcover)
Subjects: | CYAC: Frogs--Fiction. | Animals--Fiction.
Classification: LCC PZ7.D71499 Gg 2017 | DDC [E]--dc23 LC record available at
https://lccn.loc.gov/2016016406

Printed in China

1 3 5 7 9 10 8 6 4 2

The Giant Jumperee

written by
JULIA DONALDSON

illustrated by
HELEN OXENBURY

Dial Books for Young Readers

Rabbit was hopping home one day when he heard
a loud voice coming from inside his burrow.

"I'm the
GIANT JUMPEREE
and I'm scary
as can be!"

"Help! Help!" cried Rabbit.

"What's the matter, Rabbit?" asked Cat.

"There's a Giant Jumperee in
my burrow!" said Rabbit.

"Don't worry," said Cat.
"I'll slink inside and pounce on him!"

So Cat slunk up to the burrow.

But just as she was about to slink inside,
she heard a loud voice.

"I'm the
GIANT JUMPEREE
and I'll squash you
like a flea!"

"Help! Help!" meowed Cat.

"What's the matter, Cat?" asked Bear.

"There's a Giant Jumperee in
Rabbit's burrow!" said Cat.

"Don't worry," said Bear. "I'll put my big furry paw inside and knock him down."

So Bear swaggered up to the burrow.
But just as he put his big furry paw
inside, he heard a loud voice.

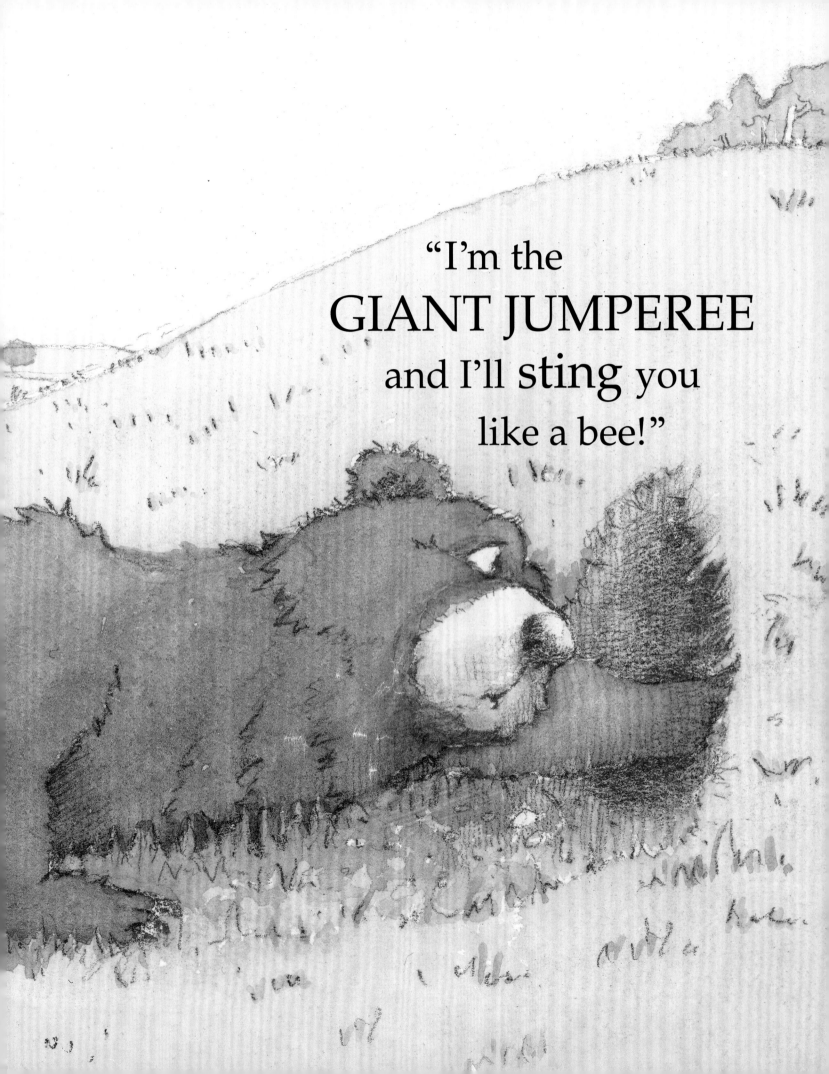

"Help! Help!" bellowed Bear.

"What's the matter, Bear?" asked Elephant.

"There's a Giant Jumperee in
Rabbit's burrow!" said Bear.

"Don't worry," said Elephant. "I'll wrap my
trunk around him and toss him away."

So Elephant stomped up to the burrow.
But just as he put his long gray trunk
inside, he heard a loud voice.

"I'm the
GIANT JUMPEREE
and I'm taller
than a tree!"

"Help! Help!" trumpeted Elephant.

"What's the matter, Elephant?" asked Mama Frog.

"There's a Giant Jumperee in
Rabbit's burrow!" said Elephant.

"Don't worry," said Mama Frog.
"I'll tell him to come out."

"No, no! Don't do that!" said all the other animals.

"He's as scary as can be," said Rabbit.

"He can squash you like
a flea," said Cat.

"He can sting you like a bee," said Bear.

"And he's taller than a tree," said Elephant.

But Mama Frog took
no notice of them . . .

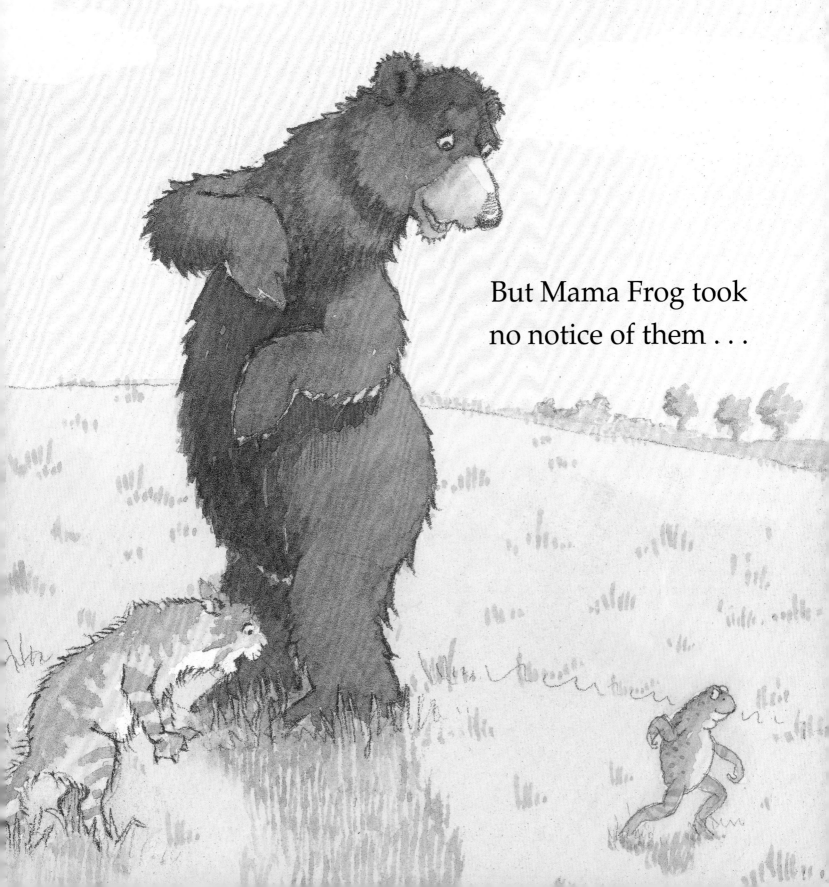

She jumped up to the burrow.

The other animals backed away.

But Mama Frog wasn't scared.

"Come on out,

GIANT JUMPEREE!" she said.
"You're the one we want to see,
so I'm counting
up to three!

"One . . .

two . . .

THREE!"

And out jumped . . .

. . . Baby Frog!

"And you're coming home for tea!"
said Mama Frog.